MYSTERY
of the LOST RING
(WITH TWO HEARTS)

Written by Robyn Supraner
Illustrated by Marsha Winborn

Troll Associates

Library of Congress Cataloging in Publication Data

Supraner, Robyn.
  Mystery of the lost ring (with two hearts)

    (A Troll easy-to-read mystery)
    Summary: Two best friends make each other gifts
but one of the gifts mysteriously disappears.
    [1. Mystery and detective stories.   2. Friend-
ship—Fiction]   I. Winborn, Marsha, ill.   II. Title.
III. Series: Troll easy-to-read mystery.
PZ7.S965Myp   [Fic]   81-7520
ISBN 0-89375-596-6 (lib. bdg.)   AACR2
ISBN 0-89375-597-4 (pbk.)

10   9   8   7   6   5   4   3

MYSTERY
of the **LOST RING**
(WITH TWO HEARTS)

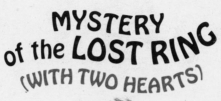

4

Heather and Florence are best friends.

They dress alike.
They walk alike.

They smile alike.
They talk alike.

They both get A in math and science.

They both get C in sewing and history.

One day Florence said, "I wish our names were more alike."

"So do I," said Heather.

So, right on the spot, Florence changed her name. She changed it to Feather. She changed it for three reasons: First of all, it sounded like Heather. Second of all, her hair was short and curly, like feathers. And third of all, she didn't like the name Florence in the first place.

So, here they are. Heather Martin and Florence McGee. Heather and Feather. Friends to the end.

One day, Heather went to the dentist. Feather had nothing to do. When Heather was there, they always did something— even when there was nothing to do.

Feather thought, "I will make a surprise for Heather. I will make something special to show we are best friends."

She thought and thought. Then, she had a wonderful idea. First, she found a spool of wire. Then she found a wire cutter. Snip. Clip. Bend. Twist. A little more here. A little less there. At last, the surprise was done.

When Heather returned from the
dentist, Feather was waiting for her.

"Did it hurt?" she asked.

"A little," said Heather.

Feather held the surprise behind her
back. "I have something that will make it
better," she said. "It is something special.
I made it myself, and it is for you."

She gave the surprise to Heather.

"A ring!" cried Heather.

"With two hearts," said Feather. "One for you and one for me. It shows we are best friends."

"It's beautiful," said Heather.

"It was very hard to make," said Feather.

"It's the most beautiful ring in the whole world," said Heather. "I will wear it forever."

The next day, Heather and Feather walked to school.

"Your new ring looks very nice," said Feather.

"I know," said Heather. "It was a surprise from my best friend."

"It must be wonderful to get a surprise from your best friend," said Feather.

"It is," said Heather. "That is why I am making a surprise for *my* best friend."

"Who in the world can that be?" asked Feather.

"You, of course," said Heather. "Who else?"

After school, Feather waited for Heather at their usual place. She waited and waited. "What can be keeping her?" thought Feather. She waited some more. Just when she was about to give up, she saw Heather.

"Where were you?" asked Feather.
Heather did not answer. Her eyes
were red and puffy. She had been crying.
"What *happened*?" asked Feather.
Heather held out her hand. The
friendship ring was gone.

"It disappeared," said Heather. "It vanished into thin air."

"Don't be silly," said Feather. "Rings do not vanish into thin air."

"Sometimes they do," said Heather. "Mine did. You probably hate me now!"

"How can you say that," said Feather. "You're my best friend. After all, it was only a ring."

"With two hearts," cried Heather. "One for you and one for me."

"And don't forget," said Feather. "It was very hard to make. It took me one whole day."

"Ooooooh!" cried Heather.

"Don't cry," said Feather. "Think. Did you take the ring off your finger?"

"Not once," said Heather. "Not even when Mary Alice wanted to try it on."

"What about Shirley?" asked Feather. "Did you let Shirley try it on?"

"Shirley didn't want to try it on."

"It wouldn't fit Shirley's fingers anyway," said Feather. "Come with me. We'll ask Mr. Sprinkle. Maybe he has your ring."

Mr. Sprinkle worked in the Lost and
Found at school. "No," he said, shaking
his head. "No one turned in a ring today.
How about a pen? I have a lot of pens.
Red pens. Blue pens. Old pens. New pens.
Are you sure you didn't lose a pen?"

"Very sure," said Heather. "I lost a
ring. It was very pretty with two hearts in
the middle."

"I made it myself," said Feather. "It
was very hard to make. It took me one
whole day."

"I'm sorry," said Mr. Sprinkle. "How about some mittens? Orange? Yellow? Pink? White? Here's a pair with funny clowns. Maybe you lost some mittens."

"No," said Heather. "It was a friendship ring."

"Boots!" cried Mr. Sprinkle. "A nice
lunch! Ah! A peanut-butter-and-jelly
sandwich with only two bites missing!"

"No," said Heather.

"No," said Feather.

"A sweater!" yelled Mr. Sprinkle.
"Think about it! Maybe you lost a
sweater!"

Heather and Feather went out and closed the door. In the hall, they could still hear Mr. Sprinkle yelling, "Here's a hat! It's just your size!"

"Let's ask the janitor," said Feather. "Maybe she found your ring."

The janitor shook her head. "No," she said. "No ring. I found a tooth today. Can you use a tooth?"

"This is important," said Feather. "It was a very valuable ring with two perfect hearts in the middle. I made it myself."

"It took her all day," said Heather, who was about to cry.

"Don't cry," said the janitor. "It was only a ring."

"It was very hard to make," said Feather.

Heather burst into tears.

"I have an idea," said the janitor. "Why don't you look through the trash? Maybe I swept it up by mistake."

Heather and Feather emptied all the trash cans. They found chewed-up bubble gum. They found candy wrappers and lollipop sticks. They found melted ice cream and a lot of crumpled paper. They did not find Heather's ring.

"Think!" said Feather. "Where were you today?"

"In the lunch room," said Heather.

"Where else?" asked Feather.

"The art room."

"And?"

"The gym and homeroom."

"Think harder," said Feather. "Were you anyplace else?"

"The bathroom," answered Heather.

"That's it!" cried Feather. "The ring slipped off your finger when you washed your hands."

"It didn't," said Heather.

"Why not?" asked Feather.

"I didn't wash my hands," said Heather.

"Well," said Feather, "we will look everyplace else. You take homeroom and the lunch room. I'll take the art room and the gym."

"No," said Heather. "*I'll* take the art room. I am making a surprise for you, and I don't want you to see it."

"A surprise?" said Feather. "For me? What is it?"

"I said it was a *surprise*," said Heather.

"Hurry," said the janitor. "The school will be closing soon."

Heather looked in the coat closet.

Feather looked behind the lunch counter.

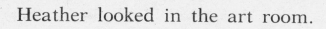
Heather looked in the art room.

Feather looked in the locker room.

They came back empty-handed.

"The school is closed," said the janitor. "You have to go home now."

"It's no use," said Heather. "My ring is gone. It vanished into the clear blue sky."

"I can't believe it," said Feather.

"Believe it," said Heather. "My ring disappeared."

The next day after school, Feather waited for Heather again. She waited and waited. "This is getting to be a habit," thought Feather. Just when she was about to give up, Heather came running down the block.

"Look what I have!" she shouted.

"Look where you're going!" Feather
shouted back.

But it was too late. *Blam!* Heather
ran, smack, right into Mary Alice.

"What do you have?" asked Feather.

"That," said Heather. She pointed to
the ground.

"What is it?" asked Feather.

"It *was* your surprise," said Heather.

"What *was* it?" asked Feather.

"It was a statue of two friends. You and me," said Heather. "It was very hard to make." She began to cry.

Feather picked up the pieces. She looked at the broken statue. "I love it," she said. "It's the most wonderful surprise in all the world."

"Maybe I can fix it," said Heather.

But Feather didn't hear her. She was jumping up and down. "Look!" she cried. "Do you see what I see?"

"My ring!" cried Heather. "It slipped off my finger and got lost in the clay. If I didn't drop the statue, I never would have found it."

"It got a little bent," said Feather.

"It doesn't matter," said Heather. "The important thing is that you made it for me."

"True," said Feather. "How very
true!"

"Let's go home," said Heather.

"Yes, let's," said Feather.

So, there they go. Heather Martin and Florence McGee. Heather and Feather. Friends to the end.